MS WIZ LOVES DRACULA

Terence Blacker has been a full-time writer since 1983. In addition to the best-selling *Ms Wiz* stories, he has written a number of books for children, including the *Hotshots* series, *The Great Denture Adventure*, *The Transfer*, *The Angel Factory* and *Homebird*.

What the reviewers have said about Ms Wiz:

"Every time I pick up a Ms Wiz, I'm totally spellbound . . . a wonderfully funny and exciting read." *Books for Keeps*

"Hilarious and hysterical." Susan Hill, *Sunday Times*

"Terence Blacker has created a splendid character in the magical Ms Wiz. Enormous fun." *The Scotsman*

"Sparkling zany humour . . . brilliantly funny." *Children's Books of the Year*

Titles in the Ms Wiz series

All *Ms Wiz* titles can be ordered at your local bookshop or are available by post from Book Service by Post (tel: 01624 675137).

Terence Blacker

Ms Wiz
Loves Dracula

Illustrated by Tony Ross

MACMILLAN
CHILDREN'S BOOKS

First published 1993 by Picadilly Press Limited
Published 1994 by Macmillan Children's Books

This edition published 1997 by Macmillan Children's Books
This edition produced 2001 for The Book People Ltd,
Hall Wood Avenue, Haydock, St Helens WA11 9UL

ISBN 0 330 34873 6

Text copyright © Terence Blacker 1992
Illustrations copyright © Tony Ross 1997

The right of Terence Blacker to be identified as the
author of this work has been asserted by him in accordance
with the Copyright, Designs and Patents Act 1988.

9 8

A CIP catalogue record for this book is available from
the British Library.

Phototypeset by Intype London
Printed by Mackays of Chatham plc, Kent

*This book is dedicated to
all the children who have written
to me about Ms Wiz.*

Acknowledgements

*I would like to thank Salvatore Genco,
Andrea Kaizer and Darren Wade of East-
field Primary School, Enfield, whose own
Ms Wiz story was the original inspiration
for this book, and all the pupils of
Mowbray County Junior School, South
Shields, for their helpful comments on the
story itself.*

CHAPTER ONE

A Load of Parents
Getting Drunk

It was the end of the last day of autumn
term at St Barnabas School. Children were
running across the playground to be met by
their parents at the school gate. From the
gym nearby could be heard the sound of a
radio playing. Tonight was the night of the
Christmas fancy-dress dance held by the
PTA, and some of the teachers were
putting up the decorations.

With their satchels slung over their
shoulders, Jack Beddows and Lizzie
Thompson stood at the doorway of the gym
and watched as Class Three's teacher, Mr
Bailey, climbed a stepladder to attach
balloons to the wall bars.

"Call themselves the Parent Teacher
Association," said Jack. "All they want to do
is prance about in fancy dress."

Lizzie smiled. "Miss Gomaz told Class Four that she was going as Teddy Edward. There's a rumour that Mr Gilbert's hired a Superman costume."

"Is it a bird? Is it a plane?" said Jack in his favourite American accent. "No, it's the head teacher of St Barnabas School in a silly suit."

"I wonder what Mr Bailey's going as," whispered Lizzie.

"A ghost, probably," said Jack. "He'd

look all right with a sheet over his head."

As if he had heard their conversation, Mr Bailey glanced over and saw the two children standing in the doorway. "Off you go, you two," he called out. "It's the grown-ups' time now."

"Bye, sir," Jack called out. "Don't forget to dance with Teddy Edward."

It was getting dark as Jack and Lizzie made their way across the school play-

ground and out of the gate towards Lizzie's house where Jack was staying that night.

"I know it's only a stupid fancy-dress dance but I really wish we were going," Jack said. "I'd give anything to see Mr Gilbert as the Man of Steel."

"And we've got Helen from next door babysitting," said Lizzie gloomily. "She's really strict about when we go to bed."

"If only we had—" Jack had been just about to say, "If only we had Ms Wiz as a babysitter," when he saw a familiar figure sitting on a wall across the road from the school. She was wearing a long overcoat and a woolly hat, but that dark hair was unmistakable. "Look who it is," he said.

"I don't believe it," said Lizzie. "She hasn't visited us for ages."

"Ms Wiz!" Jack shouted as they ran towards a zebra crossing nearby, but the figure continued to look down at the pavement, deep in thought.

"She doesn't look very happy,"

murmured Lizzie as they approached.
"Perhaps she's lost her magic."

"Yo, Ms Wiz," Jack called out.

Ms Wiz looked up, as if awakening from
a daydream. "Hi, Jack," she smiled. "Hi,
Lizzie."

"We were just talking about you," said
Jack. "I'm staying with Lizzie tonight and
we need a babysitter."

"Yeah, it's unfair," said Lizzie. "My
mum and Jack's parents are going to the

5

PTA fancy-dress dance and we have to stay at home with the world's strictest babysitter."

"Fancy dress?" Suddenly Ms Wiz looked interested. "That sounds fun."

"Nah, you'd hate it," said Jack. "It's just a load of parents getting drunk and dancing with teachers to really old sixties songs."

"Great." Ms Wiz jumped down off the wall. "Where can I get a ticket?"

Mrs Thompson was in a bad mood. Lizzie and Jack had promised not to be late back from school, and they were. The shop where she had hired a nurse's uniform for tonight's dance had promised it would fit her, and it didn't. She was looking at herself in the hall mirror when the bell rang.

"Glad you could make it," she said, opening the door to Lizzie and Jack.

Lizzie looked at her mother in the nurse's uniform. "Er, you look great, Mum," she said eventually.

"Yeah, dig Florence Nightingale," said Jack in a serious attempt at politeness.

"I look ridiculous," moaned Mrs Thompson. "I'm all . . . bulgy."

From the darkness behind Jack and Lizzie could be heard a faint humming sound.

"What's happening?" Mrs Thompson looked down at her uniform which seemed to be slowly expanding. After a few seconds, the material stopped moving. It was now a perfect fit.

"Is that any better?" asked Ms Wiz, stepping out of the shadows.

"This is Ms Wiz," said Lizzie. "You remember the Paranormal Operative who used to visit Class Three? Well, she's back and, as you can see, her magic's still working."

"Paranormal Operative? Magic?" Mrs

Thompson looked from the nurse's uniform to Ms Wiz. "The costume won't shrink back at the wrong moment, will it?" she asked nervously. "I don't want to go all bulgy again just when I'm dancing with Mr Gilbert."

Ms Wiz laughed. "No," she said. "Anyway, I'll be there to make sure the spell keeps working."

"Will you?" Mrs Thompson looked surprised.

"Ms Wiz wants to go to the dance," Lizzie explained.

"Weren't you banned once from St Barnabas?" asked Mrs Thompson. "Something about sending a class on a field trip to the other side of the world?"

Ms Wiz shrugged. "It was a long time ago. Anyway, no one will recognize me in fancy dress."

"I'm not sure." Mrs Thompson frowned as she turned towards the kitchen. "Will

you promise not to do any of your spells?"
she asked.

"Trust me," said Ms Wiz.

"Oh, all right," said Mrs Thompson.
"You can change in my room upstairs."

"But what will you change into?" Lizzie
asked.

Ms Wiz smiled. "I'll think of
something," she said.

"There's one thing I don't understand,"
said Jack, after Ms Wiz had gone to
change. "Whenever Ms Wiz comes to see
us, she tells us that she goes where magic
is needed."

"That's true," said Lizzie. "There's
always a problem that needs solving when
she turns up."

"So who is it who needs the magic
now?" asked Jack. There was silence in the
kitchen as the three of them thought about
this.

"Perhaps it's Ms Wiz herself who needs the magic," said Mrs Thompson eventually.

"Ms Wiz need magic?" Jack laughed. "Never."

"She might be lonely," said Mrs Thompson. "That would explain why she's so keen on going to the dance."

"Maybe she's looking for a boyfriend," said Lizzie.

Jack laughed. "Don't be ridiculous," he said. "Ms Wiz isn't like that – anyway she's got Herbert the rat for company."

"A rat's not quite the same as a boyfriend," said Lizzie.

"Hmm," said Mrs Thompson. "No comment."

There was a rustling sound from the stairs. A dark, wild-haired witch dressed in stylish black off-the-shoulder rags, her green eyes sparkling, made her way slowly down the stairs.

"How do I look?" asked Ms Wiz.

CHAPTER TWO

Strangers in the Night

Before Dracula arrived, it had been a PTA
dance like any other PTA dance. There was
soggy quiche. There was wine which even
Mrs Hicks, who could drink almost
anything, had difficulty in swallowing. One
of the dads had already hurt his back
doing the twist. In spite of all Mr Bailey's
efforts, the gym didn't really look like a
disco – it looked like a gym with a few
balloons hanging from the walls.

Ms Wiz stood with Lizzie's mother near
the Christmas tree. She wanted to dance
but the fathers seemed to be too nervous to
speak to her.

"I think they recognize me," she
whispered to Mrs Thompson. "They're
worried I'll bewitch them or something."

Mrs Thompson glanced at Ms Wiz. "The

trouble is we're not used to such glamorous witches at St Barnabas," she said. "We have this idea that a witch should be an old girl with a hunchback, long dirty fingernails, and a drip on the end of her crooked nose."

"How very old-fashioned," sighed Ms Wiz, smiling at a small figure in a strange costume who was now approaching them.

"Hullo, I'm the head teacher," said Mr Gilbert, shaking Ms Wiz's hand. He gave a nervous little laugh. "Except tonight I'm Superman."

"Ah yes," said Mz Wiz, who had been wondering why he was wearing blue pyjamas and a little red cape. "Pleased to meet you, Superman."

"Now, I can't help feeling we've met somewhere before," said Mr Gilbert.

"I don't think so," said Ms Wiz quickly. "My name's—"

It was at that precise moment that the music stopped and the lights went out.

There were groans from around the gym. "Not *another* power cut," said a voice in the darkness. "That's the third time the electricity's gone off this week."

Someone standing by the doorway lit a match. The door behind him opened to reveal a tall, dark figure with glittering eyes. Two long incisor teeth protruded slightly over his lower lip.

"Got a torch, Count Dracula?" laughed one of the parents.

The figure in black said nothing.

"Typical," laughed Lizzie's mother, as Mr Gilbert hurried away to find some candles. "Something like this always happens at the PTA dance. But at least it saved you from having to dance with Superman."

"Mmm?" Ms Wiz was staring across the room.

"That man's got the heaviest feet—" Mrs Thompson realized that Ms Wiz was no

14

longer listening to her. "Have you seen someone you know?"

A hint of colour had come to Ms Wiz's cheeks. "I think I've just seen the vampire of my dreams," she said.

Lizzie wasn't tired. Nor was Jack. They sat in Lizzie's room listening to the television downstairs and wondering what was happening at the PTA dance.

"My mum says that when you can't sleep, you should get up and walk around a bit," said Lizzie.

Jack thought about this for a moment. "Perhaps we could walk down the road to St Barnabas. The fresh air would do us good. We could take a look at the dance through the window of the gym."

"What about Helen, downstairs?" Lizzie whispered.

"We'll only be gone a few minutes. She's probably asleep in front of the telly."

Without another word, the two children dressed.

"This is bad," muttered Lizzie as, a few minutes later, they stood at the top of the stairs. "My mum'll kill me if she sees us."

They crept downstairs, silently lifted the spare front door key off a hook in the hall and let themselves out of the house into the dark night.

It had been one of the strangest dances she had ever been to, Lizzie's mother thought as she danced with Mr Harris. First of all, when the electricity had come back on, there had been an odd humming noise from the direction of Ms Wiz. Suddenly the lights in the gym had dimmed, giving it a soft, romantic glow.

"That's better," Ms Wiz had said. Without another word, she had walked across the room and had introduced herself to Dracula.

Then there was the music. Normally it was loud and fast at the PTA dance but, when Ms Wiz had first walked onto the dance floor with Dracula, she had glanced at the cassette player, there had been another humming noise – and, from then on, the only music the machine would play was slow, smoochy Frank Sinatra songs, to which Ms Wiz and Dracula danced all evening.

Not that the music made any difference to Mr Harris, Mrs Thompson sighed to herself. As usual, he was pushing her around the dance floor like a removal man delivering a cupboard on his last shift. Over his shoulder, Mrs Thompson smiled as she saw Dracula and Ms Wiz dancing slowly in one of the darker corners.

"It's all very strange indeed," she murmured.

"What's that, love?" Mr Harris barked in her ear.

"Um, it's strange how well you dance," said Mrs Thompson quickly.

"Oh yes, I like a good old stomp," said Mr Harris, treading hard on her right toe.

As the song ended, Ms Wiz and Dracula slipped out of the gym and into the playground.

"I'd better be going home now," said Dracula in a deep, silky voice.

"Of course," Ms Wiz smiled cheerfully. "The last train for Transylvania must be leaving soon."

"Perhaps we could, you know . . ." Dracula seemed to be lost for words. "D'you fancy going to the cinema some time?"

Ms Wiz laughed. "Afternoon show, I suppose. You must be busy at night."

"Busy?"

"Night shift. All that flying about with the other vampires."

"Yes, of course." Dracula sighed. "It does keep me busy."

For a moment, there was an awkward silence in the playground, except for the sound of "Strangers in the Night" drifting across from the gym.

"Well," said Ms Wiz softly. "It's been a great pleasure." She shook Dracula's hand and turned away.

"What did you say your name was?" Dracula called out.

"Ms Wiz. But you can call me Dolores."

"Can I telephone you?"

Ms Wiz hesitated. "I'm not on the telephone, I'm afraid," she said. "But I

suppose you could leave a message for me with Lizzie's mother, Mrs Thompson." She waved and walked into the gym.

"Who's Lizzie? Who's Mrs Thompson?" murmured Dracula to himself. "Oh, I'll never see that beautiful witch again." He took a handkerchief out of his top pocket and blew his nose. Then, slowly and sadly, he walked out of the school gates and down the road.

*

"Talk about embarrassing," said Jack, emerging from the shadows nearby. "For one moment, I thought they were going to kiss or something gross like that."

"They couldn't," said Lizzie. "His teeth would get in the way, wouldn't they?" Glancing down, she noticed a small white card on the ground. "He dropped something," she said, picking it up. "It says 'College of National Assessment'. Then there's an address. Maybe he wasn't Dracula after all."

"Of course he was," said Jack. "I mean, he wouldn't go around with cards saying 'DRACULA – VAMPIRE AND BLOODSUCKING NEEDS – ESTIMATES FREE', would he? That card's just to throw people off his track."

Lizzie was walking towards the school gate. "He seemed a bit shy for a vampire," she said.

"That was a vampire, all right," said Jack. "Can you imagine Ms Wiz dancing the night away with just an ordinary bloke in a silly fancy dress?"

"I don't know," said Lizzie. "I don't seem to know anything about Ms Wiz any more."

CHAPTER THREE

A Gorgeous, Hunky Lord
of the Undead

A low moaning sound could be heard
coming from the kitchen when Lizzie and
Jack came down to breakfast the following
morning.

"Oh no," Lizzie sighed. Mrs Thompson
was sitting at the kitchen table, her head in
her hands, staring into a cup of coffee.

"Your mum looks really ill," whispered
Jack.

"It's what's called a hangover," said
Lizzie, speaking as loudly as before.
"Every year Mum goes to the PTA dance
and every year she has this special
PTA dance hangover from drinking too
much."

"Someone must have put something in
the wine, I only had two glasses,"
muttered Mrs Thompson, as she looked up

at the children with small, bloodshot eyes.

"It's called alcohol, Mum," said Lizzie.

"Where's Ms Wiz?" asked Jack, anxious to change the subject.

"Flew home after the dance," said Mrs Thompson. She sipped at her coffee. "I think she lost her heart to Dracula."

"Her heart? Ugh, you mean he just took it?" said Jack. "Didn't it make a mess on the dance floor?"

Mrs Thompson laughed, then winced.

"No jokes," she begged. "Don't make me laugh."

"It wasn't really Dracula, was it?" asked Lizzie, thinking of the card she had picked up in the playground.

"No one knew who he was." Mrs Thompson stood up slowly. "Wasn't a parent, wasn't a teacher. Maybe Ms Wiz thought the PTA dance was a Bring Your Own Vampire party."

The front doorbell rang loudly.

"I wonder who that could be," said Lizzie.

Mrs Thompson was tottering towards the stairs. "Tell them to go away. I'm off back to bed," she muttered, as Jack and Lizzie ran to the front door.

An extraordinary sight greeted their eyes. Ms Wiz, wearing a pink T-shirt covered with purple hearts, was hovering six inches above the ground. A cloud of beautiful yellow butterflies flitted around her head.

"Jack! Lizzie!" she exclaimed in a

strange, fluting voice. "I was passing by and I just wanted to tell you that it's an absolutely *wonderful* morning."

Lizzie held the front door open as Ms Wiz floated into the house, followed by the yellow butterflies.

"Are you feeling all right, Ms Wiz?" Jack asked. "Why aren't your feet on the ground? You look all . . . weird."

"Weird? *Moi?*" Ms Wiz smiled dreamily. "I've never felt better in my life. I suppose there aren't any—" she fluttered her eyelashes "—messages for me."

"What sort of messages?" asked Lizzie.

"You know, little notes written in blood which have been popped through the letterbox. Maybe a present – a dead bat perhaps or—"

"From Dracula, you mean," said Jack.

"Dracula?" Ms Wiz smiled innocently.

"Everybody knows about you and Dracula," said Lizzie. "You were the talk of the PTA dance."

Ms Wiz flew around the hall, singing out, "My head's in a spin, my heart's on fire, I've fallen in love with a bloodsucking vampire."

"Er, Ms Wiz—" said Jack.

"We'll stay together, we'll never part, my love for Drax is like a stake through my heart."

"Ms Wiz, I think—" said Lizzie, trying to interrupt.

"Blood is red, veins are blue, his fangs are pearly and—"

"Ms Wiz!" shouted Jack. "Stop floating about the hall spouting poetry, and just think about this. You cannot fall in love with a vampire."

Ms Wiz paused mid-flight. "Why not?" she smiled. "This is the real thing at last."

"Yes, but is *he* a real thing?" asked Lizzie. "After all, you did meet him at a fancy dress dance. Maybe he's not a real vampire."

"Of course he is," Ms Wiz smiled. "I'd

know a vampire anywhere. Those cute, long nails. Those dark, sweet, evil eyes."

"All right, let's say he is Dracula," said Jack. "He's not exactly going to be a perfect boyfriend, is he? I mean, think of all that bloodsucking. After a few nights out with him, your neck would be like a pin-cushion."

Ms Wiz frowned and touched her neck nervously. Then she shrugged. "Oh, fiddle-di-dee," she said. "What's a bit of bloodsucking between friends?"

"Then there's the garlic," said Lizzie. "When you go out to a restaurant, you'll always have to worry about what's in the meal. Vampires hate garlic."

"The course of love never did run smooth," smiled Ms Wiz. "Even with a gorgeous, hunky Lord of the Undead."

"And think of Class Three," said Jack desperately. "Can you imagine how upset they'll be when they hear you're dating a vampire?"

"That's no problem," said Ms Wiz. "You can all come and visit us in Count Dracula's dark, crumbling castle in Transylvania."

Lizzie reached into the back pocket of her jeans. She didn't want to upset Ms Wiz but it was time for a bit of reality. "He doesn't actually live in Transylvania," she said. "He dropped his card in the playground. The Lord of the Undead seems to live at 43, Addison Gardens."

"The neighbours must be pleased," muttered Jack.

For the first time, Ms Wiz floated down to earth. "You . . . you have the address of my beloved?" she asked faintly. "We must go there right now."

"Promise you won't be disappointed?" asked Lizzie.

"Take me to my fanged one," said Ms Wiz, hovering by the front door.

Lizzie looked at Jack, who shrugged. "Why not?" he said.

"Oh well, it's only five minutes away," sighed Lizzie. Picking up her coat, she called up the stairs, "Mum, we're just going down the road with Ms Wiz on a love quest for a bloodsucking vampire, all right?"

"Mmmm," moaned Mrs Thompson.

43, Addison Gardens was a block of flats. Beside the door were six doorbells with names beside them. None of them was that of Count Dracula.

"It must be the top flat," said Ms Wiz. "Vampires are like bats – they live under the roof."

"We can't just ring the top bell and ask if Dracula's at home," said Lizzie.

"I'll fly up and spy through the window," suggested Ms Wiz.

While they were talking, Jack had crept to a nearby window. Now he beckoned them over urgently.

Through the window could be seen
a small room. A long, black cloak had
been thrown over a chair near the
window. Pacing backwards and forwards
was a tall, good-looking man with dark hair
and glasses. Now and then, he would
pause to look at an object on a table
nearby. They were a set of false vampire's
fangs.

"I recognize him," whispered Lizzie.
"It's the new school inspector."

"You're right," said Jack. "What was his
name? Mr Arnold – that was it. He visited
us at the beginning of term."

"A school inspector?" said Ms Wiz.

"I'm afraid so." Lizzie looked at Ms
Wiz sympathetically. "He wasn't Dracula
after all."

"Look on the bright side," said Jack.
"There'll be other vampires."

A smile had appeared once more on Ms
Wiz's face. She floated off the ground,
singing out, "Ms Wiz was blind, you were

right to correct her, her heart belongs to a school inspector."

"I don't believe it," said Jack.

CHAPTER FOUR

It's Magic or Me

Ever since Lizzie's father had left home
when she was five, Lizzie had been really
close to her mother. She liked seeing her
father at weekends but, when it came to
the real problems in her life, there was only
one person she could talk to.

"We've got a crisis, Mum," she said
as they sat watching television together
a few days later. "People have been
seeing Ms Wiz and Mr Arnold everywhere.
At the cinema. Feeding the ducks in
the park. Podge swears he saw them
walking down the High Street holding
hands."

"Nice." Mrs Thompson was half-
listening, her eyes on the screen. "I'm so
glad he wasn't a real vampire."

"But it's not right for Ms Wiz to be

hanging around the cinema and the park
It's so . . . normal."

"I told you she was lonely," said
Mrs Thompson. "Just because she does a
bit of magic now and then, it doesn't
mean she's not interested in having a
boyfriend."

"But you're not interested in having a
boyfriend," said Lizzie.

"That's because I was married to your
father," said Mrs Thompson, pursing her

lips as if she could say more but didn't want to. "He cured me of men."

"There's an idea," said Lizzie. "Perhaps I could introduce Dad to Ms Wiz on our next weekend together. Maybe he'd cure her too."

Mrs Thompson laughed. "He couldn't handle a normal person, let alone a paranormal operative with rats, china cats and weird spells." She frowned. "I wonder if Mr Arnold knows about all that."

Lizzie thought about this for a moment. Then she leapt to her feet. "Mum, you're a genius," she said, making for the door.

"Where are you going?" asked Mrs Thompson.

"I'm phoning Jack," Lizzie called over her shoulder. "I've just thought of a solution to our crisis."

Brian Arnold walked down the High Street, which was packed with Christmas shoppers. Smiling, he whistled softly to himself. He didn't think he had ever been so happy in his life.

It had been a matter of sheer luck that he had gone to the St Barnabas dance – he had only accepted Mr Gilbert's invitation out of politeness. Yet there, as if by magic, he had met the most beautiful woman in the world.

"Yes, it really was as if by magic," he had said to Ms Wiz on their first date together two days after the dance.

"It wasn't magic, it was life," Ms Wiz had replied with the merest hint of irritation in her voice. "Magic had nothing to do with it." Mr Arnold had never discovered why the word "magic" seemed to upset her so much.

There was another wonderful thing. Mr Arnold loved children – that was why he had become a school inspector – but, until recently, he had rarely been friends with them outside school hours. Ever since he had met Ms Wiz, he always seemed to be meeting children from Class Three. It was almost as if they were following him.

In fact, he was seeing some children this very afternoon. Jack and Lizzie had invited him out for a Christmas hamburger at the Big Burger Bar on the High Street. Ms Wiz had promised to meet them there.

"A lovely girlfriend. Children offering me a Christmas hamburger." Mr Arnold smiled to himself as he opened the door to the Big Burger Bar. "What a lucky man I am."

Jack and Lizzie were already sipping cokes at a corner table.

"This was an excellent idea," he said as he took his seat.

"Mum said we could buy you burgers as a sort of Christmas present," smiled Lizzie.

"Very decent of you," said Mr Arnold. "I wonder where Dolores has got to."

"Dolores?" Jack frowned. "Oh, you mean Ms Wiz. She'll probably fly in on her

vacuum cleaner – just like she did when we
first met her at St Barnabas."

"Vacuum cleaner?" The school inspector
smiled politely. "How exactly can someone
fly on a vacuum cleaner?"

"The same way as someone can turn
Podge's father into a warthog. Or Mr
Gilbert into a sheep," said Jack. "If that
someone happens to have magic powers,
like Ms Wiz has."

"Excuse me, children—" Mr Arnold

cleared his throat nervously. "Are you telling me that Dolores – er, Ms Wiz – is . . . not quite as other women?"

"Of course she's not," said Jack. "You mean she never told you? She calls herself a paranormal operative. It's a sort of modern witch." He pulled a small bottle from his pocket. "This little bottle had my appendix in it after I had an operation at the hospital – that is, until Mr Bailey, my teacher, ate it, thanks to a bit of Ms Wiz magic."

"And she's got this rat she keeps under her shirt," said Lizzie. "It ran up the leg of the last school inspector's trousers during a lesson."

Mr Arnold nodded slowly. "So that was why Mr Smith left the job in such a hurry. When I was given his job, I was told that he had problems with his nerves."

"Hi, everyone."

Lizzie, Jack and Mr Arnold turned to see Ms Wiz, waving as she made her way across the restaurant towards them.

"What's the matter?" she said, as she arrived. "You all look as if you've seen a ghost."

"Not a ghost," said Mr Arnold grimly. "But a paranormal operative."

"Ah." Ms Wiz sat down slowly. "You've heard."

"Jack and Lizzie have been telling me all about your spells."

"Thanks, Jack. Thanks, Lizzie." Ms Wiz picked up the menu, as if nothing unusual had happened. "Now, I wonder if they have anything vegetarian here," she said.

"Dolores, I must ask you a question." Mr Arnold sat forward in his seat. "Do you or do you not keep a magic rat in your underwear?"

A faint humming sound came from across the table. "Oh look!" Ms Wiz pointed behind them. "Flying hamburgers!" There were gasps from the diners as hamburgers floated off their plates to swoop around the restaurant, splashing relish, mayonnaise and tomato sauce everywhere. "Isn't that strange, Brian?"

But Mr Arnold ignored the hamburgers. "You're just making it worse by trying to put me off with some sort of conjuring trick," he said. "Tell me about the rat. Do you—?"

A crash of plates, followed by the thud of bodies hitting the ground, interrupted him. "That's odd, Brian," said Ms Wiz desperately. "The floor of the restaurant has been changed into an ice rink. Those poor waiters are falling all over the place."

"The rat, Dolores," said Mr Arnold.

As the humming noise died down, the flying hamburgers settled back onto their plates and the waiters picked themselves up off the floor. Ms Wiz sighed and reached inside her T-shirt, pulling out a small, brown rat which she put on the table. "Tell him, Herbert," she said.

"It's very simple," said the rat, in a squeaky but well-educated voice. "My name is Herbert and I am indeed a magic rat. I would like to take this opportunity to apologize profusely for running up your former colleague's trousers."

There was a scream from a nearby table. "A rat!" With a trembling hand, a woman pointed to Herbert. "And it's talking!"

"Yeah, yeah!" said Herbert, glancing casually in her direction. "Now, as I was saying—"

Mr Arnold had heard enough. He pushed back his chair and stood up. "That's it, Dolores," he said to Ms Wiz. "Call me old-fashioned but I'm not going out with someone who makes hamburgers fly off plates and goes around with talking rats in her undergarments." He backed towards the door. "You have to choose, Dolores – it's magic or me." Without another word, he blundered out of the door and into the street outside.

"Whoops," said Jack.

"I'm sorry, Ms Wiz." Lizzie laid a hand on Ms Wiz's arm. "We shouldn't have told him about your magic."

"Never mind." Ms Wiz smiled bravely. "He had to find out some time." She sighed. "Oh well, there goes my Christmas Day with Mr Arnold." She picked up Herbert and slipped him back under her T-shirt.

"Why don't you come round to us?" asked Lizzie. "Mum and I would love to see you."

"And I could bring your friends from Class Three around in the afternoon," said Jack.

Ms Wiz was staring out of the window, as if looking for Mr Arnold. "That would be lovely," she said quietly.

CHAPTER FIVE

The Last Spell of Christmas

"A party for Ms Wiz this afternoon? All her friends from Class Three there?" said Podge's father Mr Harris on Christmas morning. "No way. Yuletide is a time for families, not weird, green-eyed women with magic powers."

"But, Dad," Podge pleaded. "Everyone's going to be there. For Class Three, Ms Wiz *is* family. Lizzie and Jack say she needs cheering up."

"She's always been trouble, Ms Who'sit," said Mr Harris. "What do you think, Mother?"

Mrs Harris placed a hand on Podge's shoulders. "I think that, if you don't let him go, you'll be cooking your own turkey," she said firmly.

"Typical," grumbled Mr Harris. "Not even Christmas is safe from that woman."

*

Ms Wiz sat at the head of Mrs Thompson's table, her pale face illuminated by the Christmas tree nearby. "This is the best Christmas I've ever had," she said quietly. "Before we have tea, I'd just like to thank Lizzie and Mrs Thompson for inviting me for Christmas dinner and to all my friends in Class Three for coming to tea."

She looked around the table at the smiling faces of Lizzie, Jack, Podge, Caroline, Katrina, Carl and Nabila. "Seeing you all again has reminded me of all the strange adventures we've had together."

"But we'll be having more adventures in the future, won't we, Ms Wiz?" asked Katrina.

Before Ms Wiz could answer, Mrs Thompson appeared at the doorway, carrying a large cake, which she put down carefully in the middle of the table. Written in green on the cake's white icing were the words, "HAPPY CHRISTMAS, Ms WIZ."

"I don't know how to thank you," said
Ms Wiz.

"How about a trick?" suggested Jack.

"Yeah," the children agreed. "Trick!
Trick! Trick!" they chanted.

Ms Wiz held up her hands.

"I have an announcement to make," she
said when silence had returned to the
room. "After my recent . . . experiences
with a certain school inspector, I've decided
I want to lead a more normal life. Of course,

that . . . experience is over, but all the same I plan to get a flat somewhere around here. I'll be applying for a job as a teacher."

"Great," said Carl. "We can have magic every day."

"Well, no." Ms Wiz smiled. "The only way that I can become part of the normal world is to agree to give up magic."

There was a stunned silence.

"How exactly do you give up magic?" Nabila asked shyly. "Is there a strange ceremony with lots of Latin and chanting?"

Ms Wiz laughed. "All I have to do is—"

She was interrupted by the sound of three loud knocks coming from the hall.

Mrs Thompson frowned. "Who on earth could that be?" she said. There was silence as she walked out of the room to open the front door – followed by a blood-curdling scream.

The children stared at the sitting room door. First they saw a shadow, then a dark, cloaked figure filled the doorway, its fangs shining in the gloom.

"Yes." The voice coming from the figure was like ghostly wind rustling the leaves of an ancient oak tree. "I am Dracula." He moved slowly towards the table. "I have heard that the brotherhood of vampires has been mocked by one pretending to be the Lord of the Undead. Is this true?"

Nobody answered.

"Those who have laughed at the Undead

shall pay a terrible price," the stranger
continued.

"Is that you, M-M-Mr Arnold?" Lizzie
managed to say at last.

It was as if Dracula had heard nothing.
"First to pay—" the dark figure fixed
its eyes upon Ms Wiz, " — will be the
woman who actually danced with the
pretender."

Ms Wiz stood up slowly. "What do you
want of me?" she asked quietly.

"All I want—" Dracula sneered evilly as he moved more closely. "All I want—"

"Get some garlic from the kitchen, Mum," Lizzie said to Mrs Thompson. "We need to save Ms Wiz before it's too late."

"All I want . . . for Christmas is my two front teeth." With a pale hand, Dracula reached up to his mouth and removed his fangs. "Happy Christmas, Dolores," he said.

"Eh?" muttered Jack. "What's going on?"

Dracula took off his cloak, smiled, and put on a pair of glasses.

"I don't believe it," said Lizzie. "It was Mr Arnold all the time."

"A vampire for Christmas," said Ms Wiz, her eyes sparkling. "Just what I always wanted."

"Honestly," said Mrs Thompson. "Calls himself a school inspector and he comes round on Christmas Day to scare the

living daylights out of children.
This man's almost as odd as Ms
Wiz."

"It's why we get on so well," said Ms
Wiz.

"I just had to say I'm sorry about
walking out of the Big Burger Bar," said
Mr Arnold. "All those spells took me by
surprise."

"Hey," said Caroline. "Now Mr Arnold's
back, you won't have to give up your
magic."

As if in reply, a faint humming sound
filled the room. The lights lifted off the
Christmas tree, hovered in the air, then
made an archway over Ms Wiz.

"Listen to me, Class Three," she
said, stretching her arms out in front of
her. "On this Christmas Day, we are faced
with a choice. If you wish me to live in
your neighbourhood so that you can see me
every day, I shall have to retire from being
a paranormal operative. You have to decide

whether you like me for my magic or for myself."

"For yourself," said the children.

"But the magic helps," muttered Jack.

Ms Wiz reached into her coloured canvas bag that was nearby. She took out Hecate, her enchanted china cat, and placed it on the table. "As from now, this is but a normal china cat," she said.

She reached into her T-shirt and took out her magic rat Herbert. She gave him to Jack.

"That," she said as Herbert ran up Jack's arm to perch on his shoulder, "is now but an ordinary pet rat."

"And I—" The humming noise faded. The lights returned slowly to the Christmas tree. "As from today, I'll just be Dolores Wisdom. Only in real emergencies will I become Ms Wiz again." She smiled, first at Mr Arnold, who stood beside her, and then at the children. "Any questions?"

There was silence.

"Just one," said Podge at last. "Are we ever going to eat that Christmas cake?"

Laughing, Mrs Thompson passed Ms Wiz a knife. Everyone clapped as she cut the first slice.

"I say," a voice whispered in Jack's ear. "I'd be most awfully grateful if you slipped us a piece of that cake." It was Herbert the rat.

"Er, Ms Wiz," said Jack quietly. "I think the magic is still—"

Ms Wiz looked up and winked. "Still what, Jack?"

"Er, nothing, Dolores," said Jack.